Keeping

THE ADVENTURES OF
Little Mickey

KEEP ON GOING

Art & Story by
Mickey Smith Jr.
Creator of Little Mickey

Ally-Gator BookBites Publishing House | Lake Charles, Louisiana

Published by Ally-Gator BookBites Publishing House
1155 Ryan Street, Suite 213
Lake Charles, Louisiana 70601

Written and illustrated by Mickey Smith Jr.

Printed in the USA through Phoenix Color, Hagerstown, MD.
www.phoenixcolor.com

First Printing
ISBN 978-1-7324366-4-0

Our books are yummy!
www.ally-gatorbookbites.com

To my wife and the love of my life, Eugenia Smith,
and my children, Mikayla and William,
it's your love that inspires me to be more.

To my parents, Huber "Mickey" Smith Sr. and Emmer Smith,
you raised me and opened the door for me to become more.

To my sister Addie,
you are simply the best sister ever. I could not ask for more.

To my grandmother,
who gave me my first saxophone and an opportunity for more.

To a little town called Mossville,
even though you are gone, you'll never be forgotten because
it *still* takes a village to raise a child.

Community, family, and friends, Mossville (Moss-village),
you were so much more.

To Aunt Deloris Palms and Delissa Green,
you've been there from the start, always encouraging me more and more.

To Kendrick and Kimalee Guidry,
your support helped bring the vision to life, and yet it meant so much more.

To Rick and Donna Richard,
thank you for the belief and generosity that have provided me
this beautiful opportunity to do more.

My pastors Jerry and Hope Snider,
for reminding me that next steps and best steps always take a little more.

To everyone who over the years has inspired, educated, and encouraged me
to KEEP ON GOING, I say THANK YOU for helping me not only discover
the SOUND of my instrument in life but also to now help
others discover their SOUND in life as well.

To everyone I say . . .

THANK YOU & KEEP ON GOING!

My name is Mickey Smith Jr. I am a Louisiana educator and jazz musician. Music has taken me all over the globe. My life's journey has been a very long road. One that has taught me to **KEEP ON GOING** no matter how heavy the load.

Louisiana
Musician
&
Grammy-Finalist

Growing up as a kid in the Bayou State, I was called "Little Mickey" all day long.
I was a little kid, from a little town, who would one day grow up to play songs.
Now with that introduction aside, let's get right along.

Living in Louisiana, the birthplace of jazz,
I dreamed of playing the saxophone
In my very own band.
To **KEEP ON GOING** would mean spending
Lots of time practicing on the saxophone.
To become good, I imagined practicing
Each and every day at my home.

In order to **KEEP ON GOING** I would first need to find a saxophone to play.
A saxophone of my own that I could use every single day.
But a saxophone I did not have as I sat lost in thought and deep wonder.
But to my surprise that musical prize came from my very own grandmother!

I remember the words from Grandmother Smith . . .
She spoke with a tone that I will never forget,
"Enough with all this suspense . . .
K-E-E-P O-N G-O-I-N-G!
Because that horn will only play
When YOU start blowing!"

There I was excited and nervous, surrounded by all my family.
My sister even said "**KEEP ON GOING**" . . . as everyone waited happily.
They all knew that my first time on this saxophone
Would be something amazing, you see.

My first attempt was a collection of **amazingly** terrible,
Horrendous, and painful sounds.
Sounds that created both concern and frowns.
The solution to this problem I had no way of knowing.
How in the world could I ever **KEEP ON GOING**?

My parents, so supportive, stepped in quickly and said,
"We see something so special in you, kid!
We're just not quite sure exactly what it is . . .
But if you **KEEP ON GOING**, you'll definitely be a whiz!"

As they encouraged me, they also pointed to the front door.
When they said "**KEEP ON GOING**," they actually meant
Go outside and practice some more.

I thought my first attempt would
Receive a standing ovation
Or a shout of "ENCORE" . . .
Instead I was told from here on
Out to take my practice to
The great outdoors.

There I was standing outside my front door like a Buckingham Palace guard,
And as soon as I began to toot my horn, I was told **KEEP ON GOING** . . .
Farther into the yard!
Again, I tried to play my saxophone the best that I could,
Only to hear the words **KEEP ON GOING** across
An old country road and into the woods!

Deep in those dark, scary Louisiana woods,
My imagination became my greatest friend.
To **KEEP ON GOING** I often pretended that the squirrels and birds
Were my musical fans, saying, "Little Mickey, play it again!"
To overcome my fears, I imagined the noises they made
When they ran, flapped, and flew
Were the cheers and the applause
For the horn that I blew!

In the forest the green ash,
The live oaks, and the magnolia trees
Would sway and bend.
As I played, even the trees seemed
To dance in the wind.
Their leaves rustled to and fro
As I continued to **KEEP ON GOING**
With my musical show!

As the seasons, months, and
Years rolled by, my saxophone
Continued to improve.
As I played deep in those Louisiana woods,
I began to find my musical groove.
I wanted to **KEEP ON GOING** because
Something inside me said I should.
All that practicing I was doing
Was beginning to make me sound pretty good.

I decided to leave the forest and cross that old country road.
At the same time in the distance, a car approaching abruptly slowed.
I started to **KEEP ON GOING** but then I noticed it was Mr. Roy,
A man who had been my neighbor since I was a little boy.

My neighbor was a grumpy old man. His car would always **KEEP ON GOING** by.
Never a nice word did I hear him say. Not even a hello or a goodbye.
But on this time and on this day, he beckoned me over.
He had something that he wanted to say.

I prepared myself for the worst,
But what he said to me made my confidence grow to the point it nearly burst.
He said, "You're getting better, I see.
If you **KEEP ON GOING**, there's no telling how good you could be!"

Practice makes improvement, and my skills were indeed growing.
Soon even my family took notice of how I managed to **KEEP ON GOING**.
Inside the house there was a conversation I was unaware of,
Resulting in my parents giving the front door an open shove.

FINALLY! I MADE IT!
I was back inside the house. No longer was I to play alone.
From this point on people would say,
"**KEEP ON GOING**, Little Mickey, and play that saxophone!"

Now I share my story and play my saxophone for ALL to hear,
Inspiring others to discover the sound of their instruments
And to overcome their fears.

I do this because when I was a kid, I had absolutely no way of knowing
The value of an open door and the words . . .

KEEP

ON

GOING

About the Author

Anthony Cohill

Statistically speaking, Mickey Smith Jr. should have been a lost cause, but he is living proof of what faith, drive, and focus can produce.

Mickey has experienced first-hand the influence of family, caring teachers, and coaches. These **SOUND ADULTS** helped him to **KEEP ON GOING**.

Mickey's practice and play on the saxophone opened a door for him to defy the odds and become the first in his family to graduate from college. Today as a full-time educator and speaker, he continues to play the saxophone with enthusiasm and expertise.

After college, Mickey began public service as a teacher. Mickey does more than teach the mind; he reaches the heart. A figure in the music industry once saw Mickey instructing students and submitted his name to the Recording Academy for a nationwide competition. Mickey was a finalist for a Grammy Music Educator Award, which started for him a journey from the classroom to audiences across the country.

Mickey talks to educators in a humorous and heartwarming style about the everyday challenges they face in what he calls "The One-Eighty"—helping them to discover the sound to create 180 days of classroom instruction and harmony.

Mickey believes teaching at its best is an art form. Mickey believes that we all possess a unique "sound" that must be performed with excellence on the classroom stage called life and to the audience called the world. Mickey's story reminds us that, "Every child is one **SOUND ADULT** away from discovering their success!"

Mickey makes his home in southwest Louisiana with his wife and fellow educator Eugenia and their children, William and Mikayla.

School is at the heart of everything Mickey does.
School readings can be arranged through the **mickeysmithjr.com** website.
This book is also available for special discounts when purchased in quantity
for fundraising, educational use, or professional development.
Shopkeepers receive special pricing for resale.